LUCY'S FARM

A Stormy Night for Lucy

Mary Hooper

Illustrations by Anthony Lewis

MACMILLAN CHILDREN'S BOOKS

First published 2000 by Macmillan Children's Books
a division of Macmillan Publishers Limited
25 Eccleston Place, London SW1W 9NF
Basingstoke and Oxford
www.macmillan.co.uk

Associated companies throughout the world

ISBN 0 330 36797 8

Phototypeset by Intype London Ltd
Printed and bound in Great Britain by Mackays of Chatham plc, Kent

Titles in the LUCY'S FARM series

Coming soon

All of the LUCY'S FARM books can be ordered at your local bookshop or are available by post from Book Service by Post (tel: 01624 675137).

Chapter One

As she walked around the vast, steel barn, Lucy stopped suddenly beside a stall containing just one small, black-and-white cow. There was something about the cow's expression – something appealing . . .

"Oh, look at this heifer, Dad!" Lucy said. "She's so sweet."

Tim Tremayne peered into the stall. "You mean she's undersized," he said, running a practised eye over the animal and walking on.

Lucy and her dad were at the monthly livestock auction to buy some heifers –

1

young cows which had yet to have their first calf.

"It's not just that," Lucy said, though she couldn't have said exactly *what* it was that she liked so much about the little cow.

Her dad paused by the next pen and looked at a group of six sturdy heifers, trying to judge if they'd make good milkers.

"She's got lovely markings," Lucy went on, still by the little cow's pen. "And look at her eyelashes."

Her dad laughed. "If I was to buy cows on the strength of their eyelashes I'd be broke by the end of the year!"

"She's all on her own," Lucy said. People passed – farmers, mostly, in their muddy Barbours and wellington boots – but none of them took the slightest notice of the small cow. Lucy put out her hand to stroke the cow's nose, and she seemed to respond, gazing steadily at Lucy. "I bet she's lonely," Lucy said.

"Cows don't get lonely," said her dad.

The livestock sale was at Honley, in Devon, which was the nearest big town to the village of Bransley, where Lucy Tremayne, her mum, dad and little sister Kerry lived on Hollybrook Farm. They ran a dairy herd with fifty or so Friesian cows and a selection of other animals, including Rosie, a lamb Lucy had bottle-fed since she was minutes old, Donald, a donkey she'd rescued from the beach, a clutch of chickens, and Roger and Podger, their cross-bred collies.

Lucy loved all the farm animals and worked with them whenever she could. She knew, though, that it wasn't a good idea to get too attached to the cows, because they were only kept while they could produce a good amount of milk. This meant that every so often the old ones would be sold and new ones pur-chased. That was why Lucy and her dad were at the sales.

"Morning, Tremaynes!" a voice

3

boomed, and Lucy looked up to see their nearest neighbour, Mr Mackintyre, who had a large sheep farm just down the lane from them in Bransley.

Lucy beamed. She liked Mr Mack, as they all called him – mostly because he encouraged Lucy in adventures that her mum and dad weren't always very keen on! Today Mr Mack was wearing a tweedy suit and checked flat cap, his height, bulk and old-fashioned side-whiskers making him stand out among the rest of the dark-jacketed farmers.

"Good morning to you!" Tim Tremayne said, shaking Mr Mack's hand in greeting. "Not going into dairy stock, are you?"

"No fear. Just seeing what prices are being fetched," Mr Mack said. He gestured towards the six heifers. "Nice-looking bunch. Are they all in calf?"

Tim Tremayne nodded as the cows mooed and jostled each other, stamping their hooves on the straw in their pens. He consulted the catalogue in his hand, which gave details of all the animals and where they'd come from. "They're Lot 38 and they've come in from North Devon. I'll probably make a bid for them."

"What about this one? What about Lot 39?" Lucy asked. She was still standing by the little cow which, quiet and docile, was letting Lucy pet her. "Is she in calf too?"

Her dad looked down at his catalogue

again. Tim Tremayne was a tall, good-looking man with gingery-fair hair. Because he spent most of the year outside, he nearly always had a tan. "Yes, she is, but I don't want her, Lucy, so don't get any ideas. She's too small."

"But she's very sweet," Lucy said, and added mischievously, "couldn't she just stand in the field with a pink bow round her neck, looking pretty?"

Her dad and Mr Mack laughed. They moved on round the barn, looking at all the other stock, then Lucy and her dad went out to the refreshments stall where Lucy stood with the other farmers and had a hot pastie and a mug of tea. She didn't much like the strong, dark tea they served there, but she liked being with the other farmers and listening to the gossip. She wondered about the little cow she'd seen – Lot 39 – and hoped she would go to a nice home.

*

An hour or so later everyone at the market had had a chance to look at the animals and decide which they wanted to buy, and the selling started in the adjoining covered ring. While the farmers stood on a raised platform, the animals were driven in from the big barn and paraded in front of them.

Speaking through a microphone, the auctioneer gave the animals' details and asked for bids. Some good-natured bickering went on as certain cows failed to reach sums the auctioneer thought they were worth, or as farmers called out, "That animal's not worth fourpence!" or "That 'un needs a good feed-up!"

Although Lucy sometimes found it hard to follow the auctioneer's strange, rhythmical calling, she found it all quite exciting and was glad that this particular auction had fallen in half-term week. Her dad found no such difficulty, however, and when Lot 38 – the six heifers – were driven into the ring he listened carefully to the details and then raised his catalogue in the air to bid for them.

Lucy was excited, but she kept silent and very still so as not to detract from the serious business going on. She held her breath as the bidding went upwards between her dad and another man, and then her dad made one more bid. The other man was silent.

Rap! The auctioneer's hammer fell onto the wooden block to signify that a bid had been accepted. "Lot 38. Six heifers. Sold to Mr Tremayne!" he said.

Hurray! Lucy thought to herself.

Lucy's dad smiled, looking pleased. "I got a good deal there," he said to Lucy in a low voice. "I was prepared to pay more than that."

Lucy nodded at her dad excitedly. She knew money was sometimes short on the farm – in fact, Lucy's mum had recently started taking guests for Bed and Breakfast to try and earn a little extra. Lucy had even had to give up her big bedroom to make more room, and she hadn't been at all pleased about it – until her mum and dad had made her a lovely bedroom upstairs in the old hay barn which adjoined the house.

"We'll go out for another cuppa now," her dad said, "and then go and do the paperwork for the heifers. We can put them in the trailer and take them back with us this afternoon."

Just as Lucy and her dad were leaving the ring, though, the small heifer which Lucy had befriended was led into the ring on its own.

"Oh, look!" Lucy said, and she tugged at her dad's hand to stop him leaving. "Let's see who gets her."

"Lot 39, a single heifer, well in calf, from the Tapson farm in Tavistock," the auctioneer called. "Most of this herd has already been disposed of."

"And we can see why no one wanted

that 'un!" someone shouted in a rich Devon accent. The farmers roared with laughter.

The little cow stared around the ring, and then her eyes seemed to fix on Lucy.

"What am I bid? Start us off, someone!" the auctioneer called. "Nice little heifer. Come on, let's see your money!"

Lucy glanced up at her dad wistfully. The cow was still looking at her. *Oh, do buy me!* she seemed to be saying.

"Twenty-five pounds to start!" the auctioneer called. "Come on! She's in calf so she's worth at least that!"

"Oh, Dad!" Lucy breathed. "Can't we—"

"No, we can't!" her dad said.

"It's straight to the slaughterhouse for her if no one bids!" the auctioneer said.

"Dad! You said you'd got those heifers cheap – and you said you might buy seven or eight cows!" Lucy pleaded. "Oh, do let's have her!"

Behind them, Mr Mack touched Tim Tremayne on the shoulder. "She might be worth it as an investment," he said.

Lucy flashed a grateful glance at Mr Mack.

"Might be carrying twins," Mr Mack went on, winking at Lucy. "You never know with those little 'uns. Blessed good milkers, most of 'em."

"Straight for the chop if she doesn't get sold," the auctioneer said again.

"Dad!" Lucy said urgently.

Tim Tremayne glanced at Mr Mack. "I think you two are in league!" he muttered. He gave a sigh. "I'll probably regret this, but as I've had a good deal with the six I bought . . ."

He raised his catalogue. "I bid fifteen pounds for her!"

"Oh, thanks, Dad!" Lucy whispered, and then she shut her eyes. She couldn't bear it if anyone else put in a bid now.

"Any further bids? Now, come on, gents – someone else must want this nice little heifer."

But it seemed that no one did.

The auctioneer looked round the ring. "She's cheap at half the price, and she's going . . . going . . . gone to Mr Tremayne!" he called, tapping his hammer down smartly. "That's Lot 39."

"That's Buttercup!" said Lucy.

Chapter Two

"There! Don't you think Buttercup's pretty?" Lucy said to her best friend Bethany Brown. It was some weeks later, a Saturday in April, and the two girls were sitting on a five-bar gate watching the cows, which were busy with their favourite and only hobby – eating grass.

Beth put her head on one side, trying to see what was different about the little Friesian which was Lucy's favourite.

"She's smaller than the others," Beth said at last. "And she's mostly white . . . and I s'pose she's got a nice face . . ."

"She's just *lovely*!" Lucy said.

"Well, if you say so," Beth said uncertainly.

"She's due to calf in a couple of weeks," Lucy went on, "so she's much fatter than when Dad bought her."

"Have you got any calves now?" Beth asked. She loved animals nearly as much as Lucy did, but she lived in an ordinary house in the village without even a cat, so Lucy let her share in events at the farm as much as possible.

"We've got twin calves back in the barn," Lucy said. "They're gorgeous! We can go and feed them if you like."

"Come on then!" Beth grinned and jumped down from the gate. Lucy said goodbye to Buttercup, then they made their way up the lane to the big barn almost opposite the farmhouse. The barn was where the cows went every night after being milked in the shiny-clean milking parlour next door.

At the side of the barn was a small

sectioned-off area where the cows were taken to give birth and have a bit of peace and quiet away from the rest of the herd. The cows returned to their normal routine quite soon, but their calves would stay until they'd learned to drink from a bucket and fend for themselves.

As Lucy and Beth walked down the lane towards the barn, Lucy's mum called to them from the yard of Hollybrook Farm. The farmhouse itself was a sturdy building of soft golden stone, its front covered in roses and ivy. Julie Tremayne was slim, pretty and, that morning, was dressed in jeans and an old shirt of her husband's. Her hair was as blonde as Lucy's and she wore it pulled into an elastic band on top of her head.

"You haven't seen a chicken on your travels, have you?" she asked the two girls.

Beth and Lucy started laughing.

"Which one's missing?" Lucy asked.

"The little flecked one. Haven't seen her for days."

"That's Freckles." Lucy frowned. "Come to think of it, I haven't seen her either."

Lucy's mum glanced round and made a dash towards Kerry, who was about to stamp in a puddle. "Chick! Chick!" Kerry said, waving her arms at Bertram the cockerel and the two or three chickens

16

that were pecking around the cobble-stones.

"I think Freckles must have gone broody," Julie Tremayne said, picking up Kerry.

Beth frowned. "What does *that* mean?"

"It means she's sitting on her eggs," Lucy explained. "She wants chicks, you see, so instead of laying her eggs in the coop," – Lucy pointed to the wooden structure in the farmyard, where the chickens lived – "she's made a nest somewhere secret, hoping no one will find it and take the eggs away. Then she'll just sit on them until they hatch."

"Aaah. Dear little yellow chicks!" Beth said.

"Sometimes," Lucy's mum said. "But sometimes chickens lay their eggs in silly places – like where the fox can find them. So sometimes *he* gets the dear little yellow chicks."

"We'll keep an eye open for Freckles,"

Lucy said. "We're just going to see the calves."

"And then perhaps you can pop into the village for some shopping for me. We've got a guest coming this afternoon – a Mrs Dodkins."

"Dotkins!" Kerry said, liking the sound of it. "Dot . . . dot . . . dotkins!"

"Is she on her own?" Lucy asked.

Her mum nodded. "She hasn't got a car so she's coming by train to Honley and then getting a taxi. She's researching her ancestors or something. Bed, breakfast and evening meal for five days – and she's a vegetarian too! I haven't got a clue what I'm going to give her to eat."

Julie Tremayne pulled an anguished face and went indoors again, saying something about looking in her cookery books.

An hour or so later, Lucy and Beth had petted and fed the calves, been down to the village shops to get some things for

Lucy's mum and were on their way back. They'd taken Roger and Podger with them for the walk and the dogs were running a little way in front, sniffing and leaping on anything that moved. They were well-trained, though, so they came back to heel immediately they were called.

As a car came up behind them, Lucy whistled to the dogs and they both flattened themselves at the side of the road.

"That was a taxi. I bet it's Mrs Dodkins on her way to our farm," Lucy said. "Did you get a look at her?"

Beth nodded. "I think she had a funny hat on!"

They both giggled. "Just what you need for mucking out the animals," said Lucy.

She glanced up at the sky. It had been sunny earlier, but now dark clouds were gathering. "The weather's turning," she said. "Dad will want to get the cows milked early in case there's a storm."

"What happens in a storm, then?" Beth asked.

Lucy shrugged. "It's just that some of the animals don't like the thunder and lightning. Dad thinks they give less milk."

When they got back to the farm they saw that Lucy's dad had, indeed, brought the cows up from the field early and had started on the afternoon's milking.

In the farmhouse kitchen, an elderly lady was sitting at the big pine table enjoying a cup of tea and a slice of Lucy's mum's fruit cake. Julie Tremayne had done her hair and was wearing a denim dress. Now quite composed, she was stirring a large enamel pot containing vegetable goulash. Kerry sat in her highchair with a piece of cake in front of her, eyeing Mrs Dodkins curiously.

Lucy's mum introduced Lucy and Beth to Mrs Dodkins who – Lucy nudged Beth hard – was still wearing her hat.

It was emerald green, with a large speckled feather which curled down over one eye.

"Mrs Dodkins is researching her family history," Lucy's mum said. Seeing that Lucy and Beth weren't far off a fit of giggles, she gave them both a warning look.

"Indeed." As Mrs Dodkins spoke, the feather quivered. "Both branches of my family come from this area. I shall find my visit most interesting."

"Dotkins!" Kerry echoed. "Dot . . . dot . . . dotkins."

"Some of them are buried in the cemetery in the village," Mrs Dodkins went on, smiling at Kerry indulgently. "And I believe at one time they lived in a large manor house here."

Julie Tremayne put the casserole dish back into the Aga and turned to Mrs Dodkins. "Would that be the White House? It's the biggest house in the village. The Tregarth-Bartons live there now."

"Yes, that's the one," Mrs Dodkins said. "I shall be calling on them, of course." She popped the last piece of fruit cake into her mouth. "Now, I shall go and unpack, and then perhaps you'd kindly direct me to the village church. I'd like to start my investigations as soon as possible."

"Of course," Lucy's mum said. "Your bedroom is just at the top of the stairs on the right." She looked at Lucy meaningfully. "I'm sure Lucy will give you a hand with your case."

"No need! No need!" Mrs Dodkins said. She picked up the small navy holdall and, tail feather swaying, nodded to them all and made her way up the stairs.

Lucy's mum looked severely at the two girls, just daring them to say anything while Mrs Dodkins was still within earshot.

Lucy tiptoed to the kitchen door and closed it.

"Her hat!" Beth said, giggling.

Lucy nodded. "I think I know what's happened to Freckles!" she said, and both girls dissolved with laughter.

Chapter Three

"This is Donald the donkey," Lucy said. She rubbed the stubbly grey head which was poking over the paddock hedge and gave Donald a piece of the apple she was eating.

"Yes. I see," Mrs Dodkins said. Donald gave a snort and bobbed his head up and down. Mrs Dodkins took a step back. "Is he at all fierce?"

Lucy shook her head, ignoring the nudge from Beth who was standing beside her. "Not a bit," she said. "Donald's as gentle as anything."

"That's good," Mrs Dodkins said, taking another step back.

The new guest – Mrs Dotty, as the girls had been calling her privately – had asked to look round the farm before walking up to the church, so Lucy and Beth were introducing her to the animals. Unfortunately, Mrs Dodkins was still wearing the unsuitable clothes she'd arrived in – including the feathered hat.

"That's Rosie!" Lucy pointed further down the paddock where a group of sheep stood steadily eating grass. "She's smaller than the others." Lucy clapped her hands. "Rosie! Rosie!" she called, and the almost-grown lamb raced up the field towards her, Rosie's stick-like legs working like pistons under the heap of creamy wool.

Beth laughed. "She runs to you like a dog!"

"She's going to need shearing soon," Lucy said, giving the lamb some apple. "I wonder how she'll like that." She glanced at her watch. "It's five o'clock, and supper's usually at six-thirty," she said politely to Mrs Dodkins, "so if you want to go up to the church, we should go now."

"I'd better be going home," Beth said. "You can leave me at the war memorial. I won't come to the church with you." Beth gave Lucy another nudge. *She* wasn't going to be seen with Mrs Dotty more than she could help. Especially while the elderly lady was wearing that hat!

They said goodbye to the animals and then walked back to the farmhouse. Beth went inside to get her jacket, and Mrs Dotty also went inside to collect the paperwork she needed to get on with the task of tracing her ancestors.

"I should take your jacket, Lucy," her mum said, coming to the door with Lucy's green anorak. "It's starting to rain." She turned to smile at Mrs Dodkins. "Can we lend you a pair of wellies or a raincoat? When it rains, that lane turns into an absolute bog."

"Oh, I'll be perfectly all right," Mrs Dodkins said, stepping through the lobby. "April showers! One isn't bothered by them." She went out into the yard and crossed to the little hay barn opposite. "I thought I saw a cat just now."

Lucy pulled on her anorak. "You probably did," she said. "We've usually got two or three around the place." She went over to the hay barn and pointed upwards.

"My bedroom's here," she said to Mrs Dodkins. "Up the ladder and through the trapdoor."

"How novel!" Mrs Dodkins said.

"One of the best things about it is that Kerry can't get to me," Lucy said. Although Lucy loved her little sister, Kerry was awfully good at screwing up homework and leaving sticky fingermarks on whatever she touched.

Lucy, Beth and Mrs Dodkins set off up Embrook Lane. As they did so, Tim Tremayne emerged from the milking parlour, looking tired and rather grubby. As he walked towards them, a rich, cow-like smell seemed to come from him.

"My dad!" Lucy said. She grinned at him. "This is Mrs Dot . . . Dodkins," she said. "We're just going up to the church so she can look at her ancestors."

Lucy's dad wiped a hand on his dungarees and offered it to Mrs Dodkins, but she didn't seem to see it. "Delighted to meet you!" she trilled. "But we really must be going."

A bit later, Lucy was standing in the churchyard amid the dripping trees, stamping her feet to keep them warm. Mrs Dodkins had been inside the church for about half an hour now, examining memorials on the wall and copying things down, looking at carvings on the wooden pews and staring at stained-glass windows. Lucy couldn't see what could possibly interest her for so long.

Lucy had stayed inside for a while where at least it wasn't raining, but then, bored to tears, she'd come out to see what wildlife was around. She'd heard an owl, glimpsed a couple of bats and seen three squirrels digging holes in the ground – to try and find nuts they'd buried last autumn, she thought – but now she was hungry and wanted to go home.

She pushed open the heavy church door.

"Have you finished yet, Mrs Dodkins?" she asked.

"Finished for now." Mrs Dodkins came towards her, beaming. "I've found some marvellous inscriptions – some of them directly relating to members of my family."

Lucy nodded and tried to look interested.

"I shall come back tomorrow and ask the vicar to show me the parish records."

They went out of the church and down the path. Mrs Dodkins looked up at the dense, dark trees. "There are always yew trees in a churchyard, did you know that?" she said. "It used to be thought that they kept away witches." She paused by the lychgate and looked up at some carvings. "Most interesting. There's a skull carved here over the gate. This is where the coffin-bearers used to stop and rest their load on their way to bury someone."

Lucy shivered. "We'd better get going," she said. "It's really starting to pour now."

"Ah, yes," said Mrs Dodkins. "Maybe I should have accepted your mother's kind offer of a mackintosh."

By the time they turned into the yard of Hollybrook Farm, Mrs Dodkins's thin jacket was soaked through and the feather on her hat was flat to her head. Lucy ran across the yard to push open the farmhouse door and, to her surprise, found her mum and dad standing in the boot lobby, getting into their coats.

"What's up?" Lucy said, astonished. "Are you going out?"

"Oh, thank goodness you're back!" her mum said, and Lucy could see at a glance that she'd been crying.

"What on earth's the matter?"

"It's Kerry," her dad said briefly. "She's had a nasty fall. Went up the stairs and fell over backwards." He took a deep breath. "We think she may have broken her leg and . . . well, now she's gone to sleep so I think she may have concussion – that's where you have a blow to the head which knocks you out," he explained.

"Oh, no!" Lucy said, feeling like bursting into tears herself.

"We've rung Doctor Martin," Lucy's mum went on. "He said to take her straight into the hospital at Exeter. She can have X-rays there."

"The thing is," her dad said, "do you think you two will be able to hold the fort here? We shouldn't be too long. The doctor's phoned ahead to tell them we're coming."

"We're so sorry to spring this on you on the first day of your holiday," Lucy's mum said to Mrs Dodkins, "but we should be back within two or three hours."

"That's perfectly all right!" Mrs Dodkins said. "Young Lucy and I will manage admirably."

"All the animals are bedded down," Lucy's dad said. "You can do a check later if you like, Lucy – especially if the wind gets up. None of the cows are due to calve for a couple of weeks and that one with mastitis is better now, so you've nothing to worry about there."

Lucy nodded. She'd been on the evening round with her dad loads of times, so she knew what she had to look out for.

"Mr Mack's just down the lane if you

want him," Lucy's mum said worriedly. "And the dogs will look after you."

"We'll be all right, Mum!" Lucy said. "But where's Kerry?"

Lucy's dad went into the sitting room and brought out Kerry, who was wrapped up in a duvet and seemed to be sleeping peacefully.

"We'll ring when we get there – we've got the mobile," Julie Tremayne said. "Supper's in the Aga. And there's some home-made bread in the crock. Are you sure—"

"We'll be fine! Don't worry about a thing," Mrs Dodkins said, while Lucy gave her mum and dad a hurried, worried kiss. "I'm used to babysitting."

Lucy glanced indignantly at Mrs Dodkins. Babysitting, indeed! She didn't say anything, though. She was too polite – and also much too worried about her little sister.

Chapter Four

So far, so good, Lucy thought, as she and Mrs Dodkins put away the last of the supper things. Mrs Dotty hadn't done anything *too* dotty. And at least she'd changed into corduroy trousers and taken off the feathered hat!

Thoughtfully, Lucy took some dog biscuits out to Roger and Podger. They each had a big wickerwork basket out in the boot lobby, but now both were lying squashed into the same one. She filled their food bowl, gave them each a pat and took a deep breath which turned into a sigh. Glancing at her watch, she saw that it was nearly eight o'clock. Her dad, mum and Kerry had been gone an hour and a half and she didn't know what was happening. Had they seen a doctor yet? Had the hospital decided to keep Kerry in? What time would they be back? She knew someone would ring as soon as they had anything definite to tell her, but still . . .

Biting her lip worriedly, she went back into the kitchen. "Now, shall we go into the sitting room and make ourselves comfortable?" Mrs Dodkins said. "I want to write some notes on the discoveries I've made in your delightful church. Perhaps you'd like to keep me company and watch TV."

Lucy nodded. "I will," she said. "But I'd better just go and check on the animals first."

"Do you really need to go out in the rain again?" Mrs Dodkins said. She looked at Lucy, bemused. "What on earth can the animals do to get themselves in trouble?"

Lucy smiled. "It's more to check on gates and padlocks and things," she said. She looked out of the kitchen window. "I thought I'd have a look for Freckles too. She's a chicken that's gone missing. Mum's worried she'll make a nice meal for a passing fox."

"What – a takeaway chicken dinner?" Mrs Dodkins said.

Laughing, Lucy went out to the lobby. She put on her boots and rain mac and took down a torch from the shelf. Realizing there was a walk in the offing, Roger and Podger jumped up to go with her.

"Won't be long!" she called. Putting up her hood, Lucy went across the yard and into the lane. It was still raining steadily, and there was a wind blowing up. Looking down the lane towards Mr Mack's farm, she could see the row of

trees on the horizon shaking, swaying and sometimes being almost flattened by the wind.

Rosie and the rest of the sheep were fine. Safe in their small fenced enclosure within the paddock, most of them were dozing, not caring a bit that there was a storm brewing. Donald was safe too, snug under his waterproof blanket and standing immobile at the other end of the paddock.

Lucy crept away, flashing her torch under hedges as she went just in case she could see Freckles. Lucy knew that unless some harm had already come to her, the chicken was probably sitting on her eggs somewhere nearby.

Splashing through puddles, with Roger and Podger running in front of her, Lucy walked up to the big steel barn where the cows were. Leaving the dogs outside, she went in and stood on the iron railing which sectioned off part of the barn. She stretched up tall so that she could see all the cows properly.

Yes, they all seemed fine, except . . . Lucy's gaze fell on Buttercup. Her dad was always laughing about how she was able to pick out Buttercup in a field of fifty seemingly identical cows, and it was true – she could. Buttercup was by herself, some distance away from the other cows. Her head was down and she was plodding her feet up and down on the spot.

Picking her way through the slurry and straw on the floor, Lucy went over to Buttercup.

"Are you all right?" she asked, patting the little cow on the flank. Buttercup stopped stamping as Lucy stroked her and seemed to calm down a little.

"Maybe you can hear the storm outside," Lucy said. "Maybe that's what's upsetting you."

Yes, maybe it was the storm and not

the other possibility – that Buttercup was about to have her calf. Lucy just didn't want to think about *that* at the moment.

Lucy went back to the farmhouse, hoping to hear that someone had rung. There was no news, though.

"You know they can't use mobile phones in hospitals," Mrs Dodkins said. "It interferes with the doctors' pagers, I believe. And half the time the coin-operated telephones aren't working in those places."

"I suppose not," Lucy said. She put the TV on. It was nine o'clock. Maybe they were on their way home now.

Mrs Dodkins, who was bent over her papers at the table, suddenly gave a little scream. "My silver pen! It's not here!"

Lucy looked over at her.

"I've got a beautiful silver fountain pen which was an heirloom from my dear grandfather. I use it to ink in the names on my family tree."

"Have you left it at home?" Lucy asked.

Mrs Dodkins shook her head. "I had it in the church. It's usually in a holder inside my leather writing case!" She clutched the silk scarf at her neck. "But now I come to think of it, I remember hearing a little noise when I was leaving the church. I think I dropped it in the porch!"

"Oh dear," Lucy said. "Well, we can go down first thing in the morning to find it. Immediately after breakfast."

"Oh no!" Mrs Dodkins said. "I can't leave it that long. Not overnight. Someone might find it and steal it!"

"I'm sure no one will be going in the church tonight—" Lucy began, but Mrs Dodkins was already on her feet.

"Now, can you lend me some wellington boots and a mackintosh?" the elderly lady said. "I'll wrap up, take a brolly and be back before you know it."

Lucy stared at her in astonishment. "You can't go out now!" she said. "You'll get soaked. It's raining even harder than before."

But Mrs Dodkins took no notice. "Down the lane, left at the war memorial and across the green, if I remember," she said. "Shall I take one of the dogs with me?"

"Er . . . yes. If you like," Lucy said helplessly.

Lucy followed Mrs Dodkins into the lobby and stared as she got into Lucy's mum's wellington boots and her dad's yellow oilskin coat. If Lucy's mum and dad were here they'd have stopped the old lady, or taken her down to the church in the Land Rover, but Lucy on her own couldn't do a thing.

"Here we are," Mrs Dodkins said, pulling Tim Tremayne's oilskin hat well down over her grey hair. "Ready for anything!"

The sight of Mrs Dotty looking as if she was going to a fancy-dress party would have made Lucy laugh if she hadn't been feeling so worried.

Podger was roused, the front door was opened, and Mrs Dodkins and dog set off. Lucy watched them as they crossed the yard, saw the umbrella blown inside out before they'd got to the five-bar gate, and went back indoors, nibbling her bottom lip. Should she telephone Mr Mack, she wondered? But no, there was nothing to worry about yet – she had nothing to tell him. Mrs Dotty would be back soon, and so would her mum and dad, and then everything would be back to normal.

At nine forty-five, Lucy was back in the lobby, reluctantly getting into her mac and wellies. Mrs Dodkins had been gone ages – and it was only a ten-minute walk down to the village. What *could* have happened to her? She'd tried to ring her mum and dad to ask their advice, but their mobile was still switched off.

She opened the front door. "Mrs Dotty – where on earth are you?" she muttered. Mrs Dodkins couldn't have got lost – Podger knew his way home blindfolded. So where *was* she?

As Lucy opened the front door fully, the wind blew hard and almost snatched it out of her hands. Ominously, she saw flashes of lightning down towards the sea and heard distant thunder. She tucked her hair inside her hood and set off with Roger and a torch. She hadn't gone far down the lane when she heard a loud clucking coming from the hedge.

She whistled Roger to come back again. One of the chickens must have escaped from the coop, she thought. Or it might even be . . . Lucy bent low, pushed aside some pieces of hedge and shone her torch through. "Freckles!" she said.

Cluck . . . cluck . . . cluck! A very wet,

speckled chicken sat there on what looked like a bed of twigs and leaves. Lucy put her hand underneath the hen, felt around and counted. Ten eggs! And all quite warm.

"You funny broody old thing!" Lucy said. A rush of rainwater came down the bank behind the chicken and dislodged some of the twigs from the makeshift nest.

"Yes, I can see what's going to happen," Lucy muttered. "You and your eggs are going to get washed away." She sighed.

"I suppose I'll have to put you somewhere safe."

She thought quickly, then scooped up the nest and eggs, dislodging Freckles. Holding the nest together as best she could, and with the hen squawking indignantly at her heels, Lucy carefully made her way back to the farmyard.

"Yes, I know you don't like it, Freckles," Lucy said, "but you should have laid your eggs somewhere sensible, shouldn't you?"

Lucy went into the hay barn and put the nest of eggs in a corner on the floor. Then she looked at the soaking wet chicken. "You're not going to be much good at keeping those eggs warm, are you?" she said. "I suppose I ought to fix up some sort of incubator."

An incubator was a special, warm box where eggs could hatch out, and Lucy had seen her dad construct a makeshift one more than once. He'd put a table lamp in a cardboard box, then put the ready-to-hatch eggs underneath the light to keep them warm.

Quickly, Lucy ran up the stepladder to her room and brought down her table lamp. Luckily, it had a long lead which ran all the way back upstairs. She found an old cardboard box and then put lamp, nest, eggs and chicken inside.

She switched on the lamp. "There!" she said with satisfaction. "Stay there, Freckles, and you can all keep warm together."

Cluck . . . *cluck* came from Freckles, who was turning herself round and round on the eggs and looking very content indeed.

Lucy whistled for Roger, who was in a corner of the hay barn looking for cats. "Come on," she said. "You and I have got to go and find Mrs Dotty."

Chapter Five

"Hello! Are you there, Mrs Dodkins?" Lucy pushed open the small gate leading into the churchyard and shone her torch up the path. The wet tombstones gleamed as the torchlight struck them, and Lucy shivered. She'd never liked churchyards – especially not on dark, wet nights like this, with the wind howling eerily through the trees.

"Hello! Mrs Dodkins!" she called again. She paused to listen for an answer, but all she could hear was the rain lashing down and the wind gusting.

Lucy bent her head against the driving rain and went further up the gravel path, holding onto Roger's collar with her free hand. She was sure the church itself would be locked at night, so she didn't think Mrs Dodkins could be inside. So where *was* she?

"Oh, help! Help me someone!" As Lucy neared the porch, she heard a faint cry and shone the torch ahead of her. Across the doorway of the church, to prevent birds from roosting in the porch, was a wire outer door. This was closed tight, but inside, her hands gripping the wire, was a terrified-looking Mrs Dodkins. Podger sat beside her, looking slightly bemused.

"Oh, help! I'm trapped inside and there's a strange creature in here with me!" she cried.

Lucy let go of Roger, tucked the torch under her arm and pulled hard at the door. It was stuck fast, though, and didn't move.

"What happened?" Lucy asked. "How did you get in here?"

Mrs Dodkins gave a shaky wail of fright. "I came in the porch and found my pen, and was just about to go out when something huge and white swooped down on me. I screamed – and as I did so a gust of wind slammed this door shut so I couldn't get out!" She looked over her shoulder fearfully. "That white thing is in here with me now. It's making a low, mournful sound – I think it's some sort of spirit creature!"

Lucy shone her torch behind Mrs Dodkins and up to the wooden eaves of the porch. A beautiful white owl was sitting there, looking calmly down on them. "*Whoo-whoo* . . ." it said, blinking its eyes in the light.

"It's an owl!" Lucy cried. "A lovely big white owl."

"Oh, surely not," Mrs Dodkins said, peering upwards and starting to look rather embarrassed.

"It's gorgeous. I've never seen one so close before."

"Never mind about that, dear," Mrs Dodkins said uneasily. "Just get me out."

Lucy pushed, shook and, in the end, kicked the door until it gave way. Podger ran out to join Roger, and Mrs Dodkins fell on Lucy with cries of joy. "Rescued! Oh, I'm so grateful!"

Lucy smiled. Strange, funny old Mrs

Dotty. "Have you got the pen put away safely now?" she asked.

Mrs Dodkins nodded. "In my pocket." She glanced up at the owl again and rammed her oilskin hat more securely on her head. "Just an owl, eh? For goodness' sake let's go home!"

As they came through the farmhouse door, the phone was ringing. Lucy dashed to answer it, her wet boots leaving damp puddles all over the tiled floor.

"Lucy. Are you all right, darling?" her mum's voice asked.

Lucy breathed a sigh of relief. "Yes. fine," she said. She wouldn't tell her mum about Mrs Dotty's adventure just at the moment, she decided. "But what's happening? Are you on your way home?"

"Yes, thank goodness. We're just leaving the hospital now."

"And what about Kerry? Is she all right?"

"Kerry's fine. She's broken a bone in her leg but it's all quite straightforward and she's been plastered up. She's wide awake now and isn't in any pain."

"Brilliant!" Lucy said.

"Is everything all right? Did you manage supper?"

Mrs Dodkins passed the doorway and waved to Lucy. "Just going to have a bath," she said cheerily, as if nothing had happened. "Everything OK with your little sister?"

Lucy nodded to her. "Everything's fine." She spoke to her mum again. "Supper was OK and – did you hear that? – Mrs Dotty's going up to have a bath."

"I hope there'll be enough hot water," her mum said. "How's the storm?"

"Raging," Lucy said. "Trees swaying, rain pouring, thunder and lightning and everything."

"It's the same here," her mum said. "Tuck up warm and see you soon!"

Lucy blew kisses to everyone before putting down the phone, then decided, before she got out of her wet things, that she ought to go and check on Buttercup. She could tell her dad the latest as soon as he came in, then.

Leaving the dogs scrambling to get in the same basket, Lucy took the torch and left the farmhouse again. She was worried about Buttercup. Surely the little cow couldn't be about to have her calf. Could she?

Over in the barn the cows were almost silent, steadily chomping their feed or dozing in the darkness. One cow, though, wasn't silent. One cow was plodding round and round in circles, making little noises and looking uncomfortable. Buttercup.

Lucy looked at the little cow and sighed. "I thought so," she muttered. "I *thought* you might be in labour." She went over to

Buttercup and patted her. "You're not supposed to have your calf for another couple of weeks," she said. "And I wish you hadn't chosen tonight. But you'll be all right . . ." Lucy knew that most cows had their calves perfectly naturally, without any outside help, and that Buttercup had already been checked by the vet and pronounced fit and healthy. "Dad will be home soon. He'll keep an eye on you."

Buttercup gave a little bellow, as if to say, *don't leave me . . .*

"I'll tell you what," Lucy said thoughtfully. "Why don't I take you across to the hay barn to be near me. You can be quiet and peaceful in there."

Taking a length of rope, Lucy looped it round Buttercup's neck and led her through the buffeting wind across the lane and into the hay barn. The rain lashed down, plastering Lucy's hair to her face and blowing down twigs and leaves from nearby trees. Fighting her way along, Lucy thought it was the worst storm she could ever remember.

Tying the little cow loosely to a ring on the wall, Lucy got her a bucket of water and then broke up a bale of straw and strewed it over the cobblestones. "To make it a bit cosier if you want to lie down," she said, stroking Buttercup comfortingly.

She peered into the makeshift incubator. Freckles was looking warm and cosy under the light, her feathers fluffed out over her eggs. "Doing OK?" she said to the chicken, and then she giggled to herself, thinking that it was like a maternity ward in there!

Lightning flashed suddenly, and Buttercup gave a sudden bellow, making Lucy jump.

"Settle down," Lucy said, patting the cow's head. "My dad will be home soon – and by tomorrow you'll have a gorgeous baby calf."

Lucy ran back across the farmyard in the teeming rain. She'd just got her boots off and had grabbed a towel to dry her hair, when the phone started ringing.

"I'm afraid it's us again," said her mum, sounding worried. She said something else, but the line crackled and went dead for a moment, making Lucy miss half of what her mum was trying to say.

"I didn't hear that!"

"No, I'm afraid the battery on this mobile's going," her mum said. "Now, listen carefully, darling. There's a tree blown down across the road and we can't get through."

Lucy gave a frightened gasp.

"It's OK, no one's hurt, but the front of the Land Rover's got a big dent in it and we've got to wait for the emergency vehicles to arrive and shift the tree. We may not get home until the early hours of the morning."

Lucy felt a moment's panic but knew she mustn't let her mum know that. Her mum had enough to worry about.

"Are you still there?" her mum asked anxiously.

"Yes," Lucy said. She took a deep breath. "I'm OK. We'll be OK here."

"Look, what I want you to do is ring Mr Mack straight away and tell him that you and Mrs Dodkins are on your own. I'm sure he'll come down and see that everything's all right. Then you can go to bed, and before you know it we'll be home."

Lucy wondered for a moment whether she ought to tell them about Buttercup, and decided against it. Mr Mack would know what to do.

"I'd ring him myself but this battery's almost gone," Julie Tremayne went on, her voice fading. "Take care, darling. We'll be—"

The line went completely dead and Lucy put the phone down.

"Everything all right, dear?" Mrs Dodkins called from the top of the stairs and, without waiting for a reply, added, "I've had a lovely bath but I'm terribly tired so I'm going to bed. Goodnight!"

"Goodnight!" Lucy called back. "Sleep well."

The wind was lashing the rain against the kitchen windows and there was a brilliant flash of lightning from outside, followed by a heavy crack of thunder. The storm seemed to be right over them.

"It's a good job I'm not frightened of storms," Lucy muttered to herself.

She put the kettle on the Aga plate to make herself a hot drink, and then ran her finger down the list of most-used phone numbers pinned on the kitchen wall. She'd ring Mr Mack, pass on her mum's message and tell him about Buttercup. He'd know what to do. He'd come rushing up in his Land Rover and sort things out.

She picked up the phone, but instead of a dialling tone there was total silence. She jiggled the phone rest up and down, frowning deeply.

But there was no sound at all. The phone line was dead.

Lucy gave a frightened gulp. The storm must have brought down the telephone cables. *Now* what was she going to do?

Chapter Six

Lucy sat for some moments, thinking deeply, wondering what she ought to do for the best. She could run down the road and fetch Mr Mack, but she didn't like the thought of setting off down the dark lane again in the middle of a storm. Suppose Mr Mack was out when she got there? Suppose a tree blew down on her in the lane and no one found her until morning? That would leave the farm untended and Mrs Dotty on her own. Not only that, but Buttercup would be alone too.

No, she'd just have to manage as best she could. She'd seen enough calves born to know what to do – if she had to do anything – and maybe Buttercup would be a long time in labour, and her dad would be home by then anyway. If he wasn't, then maybe the phone lines would get repaired and she could reach Mr Mack. No need to panic, Lucy thought, beginning to panic anyway.

She made herself a hot chocolate drink and grabbed a slice of her mum's apple cake from the larder. She looked at her watch: eleven o'clock – she was practically having a midnight feast! Once she'd eaten the cake, she went round the house making sure the windows were shut tightly and that there were no leaks coming through the roof. Listening outside Mrs Dodkins's door, Lucy was pleased to hear a growling snore which told her that their guest was fast asleep. Just as well – she couldn't see Mrs Dotty being much use at the emergency birth of a calf!

Lucy went back to the warm kitchen

and sat by the Aga for a while with her feet inside the warming pan drawer – something her mum never let her do when she was around. The picture of poor Buttercup in the hay barn just wouldn't leave her mind, though. She *had* to go out and see how the little cow was getting on. Lucy put on an extra jumper and then her dad's Barbour – partly for luck and partly because she thought the animals would know the smell of it and find it comforting – and ran across to the hay barn, taking the big free-standing lamp with her. Roger and Podger were fast asleep now and didn't even lift their heads at all the comings and goings.

In the hay barn, Lucy found poor Buttercup in a bit of a state, panting fast and giving a distressed bellow every so often. Lucy positioned the lamp, lifted Buttercup's tail and looked at her rear to see if she could see any sign of the calf. No. There was nothing.

The cow turned to look at Lucy – a look that seemed to say, *Help me. Please!* Buttercup gave another bellow of pain.

"Oh no . . ." Lucy muttered. She'd seen all sorts of births on the farm. She'd even seen the vet deliver a calf by Caesarian, where he'd had to make a cut in the cow's tummy to get the calf out. Although each birth was slightly different, Lucy knew that what usually happened was that the baby calf's two front hooves would show in the birth canal first, followed by its head. Once those were out, the rest of the calf usually just slithered through.

But sometimes a calf would get stuck on the way, and then it had to be helped . . .

While Lucy was standing there thinking, stroking Buttercup's flank, there was a faint cheep-cheeping from the direction of the cardboard box. Going over to it, Lucy saw two tiny yellow chicks peering through Freckles's feathers.

She smiled. "*You* don't need any help then!" she said to Freckles.

The chicken gazed up at her unblinkingly, hardly seeming aware of the chicks moving beneath her. She had eight more eggs and she wanted to make sure they all hatched that night.

Lucy put out her little finger and touched the yellow fluff of a chick. It was so very soft that she couldn't feel it on her finger. "I'd better find you some maize or something," she said, although she knew that for the time being the chicks would be perfectly all right with the nourishment they'd received from inside the egg. "But I've got to sort out Buttercup first."

An enormous bellow from the cow made her jump. "I haven't forgotten you," Lucy said. "I'm thinking what I should do."

The cow was giving continuous little snorts of pain now, stamping her back legs up and down on the straw and turning in small circles. Lucy knew that cows always gave birth standing up, and that Buttercup was trying – and failing – to find a position in which she felt more comfortable.

Did Dad have any books on the birth of a calf, Lucy wondered? She didn't think so – her dad had been delivering calves since he was a boy and had no need of instruction books. But Lucy thought she might as well go back indoors and have a look anyway, and while she was there she could try the phone.

Once again she ran back to the farm-house. The rain was pelting down, the wind was howling, the cobblestones were slippery and there was a deep puddle by the door. Lucy was pleased that she'd thought to move Buttercup closer and that at least she wasn't running backwards and forwards from the barn.

In the kitchen, Lucy tried the phone again. Nothing! Then she went into the sitting room and looked along the rows of dusty books. They'd been there ever since she could remember, and she couldn't recall anyone even taking one down.

Accountancy for Farmers, *Navigating Britain's Waterways*, *Steam Engines*. No, it was as she'd thought – books on almost every subject anyone could think of, but nothing on farming or livestock. Her dad kept all his knowledge in his head.

Well, she was just going to have to do the best she could.

Fearing it was going to be a long night,

Lucy ate another slice of apple cake. Then she picked up her dad's old shirt, which her mum had left over the back of a chair. She was just about to go back outside again when she remembered something else: *rubber gloves*. The vet always wore them. She found a new pair of her mum's under the sink and took them out with her.

Back in the hay barn, Lucy looked into the cardboard box and saw there were now four chicks. "Well done!" she said to Freckles. "Only six more to go."

The chicken clucked at her – a low, contented sound. *She* was doing all right.

Unlike poor Buttercup. Lucy looked at the little cow, which was churning around as before and nodding her head up and down whilst giving short bellows of pain. "Not like you, Buttercup," Lucy said. She bit her lip. "I think I'm going to have to help you with this calf."

She took off the unwieldy, stiff Barbour and put on her dad's old shirt, which covered her like a long overall. She rolled up the sleeves, then put on her mum's rubber gloves. Now she was ready for anything.

She took a deep breath, moved the lamp around slightly and lifted Buttercup's tail.

"Yes!" she breathed. Further back, just inside Buttercup, she could see two small black hooves.

Buttercup gave another roar of pain and strained, pushing to give birth to her calf. The hooves didn't move though. They seemed to be lodged, stuck in the birth canal.

"So near . . ." Lucy murmured. She patted Buttercup and made some comforting sounds. "It's all right. You'll be OK. Just a few more pushes . . ."

But although Buttercup pushed and pushed again, the hooves didn't budge and there was no sign of the baby calf's head.

Lucy was suddenly scared. She knew she had to do something. She knew that if the calf couldn't be born because of some obstruction, then the consequences could be fatal for both cow and calf. Nothing must happen to her Buttercup!

"Somehow," she muttered, "somehow your calf has got to come out, Buttercup."

Taking a deep breath, Lucy gingerly pushed the two black hooves she could see, moving them in a little and backwards to dislodge them from whatever they were stuck against, and ease their passage through. Buttercup gave another bellow and then suddenly, miraculously, the hooves moved forward and the calf's stick-like front legs could be seen, its flattened head lying between them.

"Good girl, Buttercup!" Lucy cried. "Keep going!" She was terribly excited now – and absolutely terrified – her heart hammering and her breath ragged in her throat. "We're nearly there. Oh, keep going!"

Buttercup gave another great heave and another bellow and suddenly, all in a rush, the rest of the calf emerged, dropping and crumpling onto the straw. It had the familiar black-and-white Friesian markings, a bright pink nose and a very long tail.

Lucy gave a great sigh and burst into tears of relief. "Oh, Buttercup!" she said. "You've done it. *We've* done it!" Breathing deeply, legs shaky, Lucy moved to one side and leant against the wall. She knew her job was done, and that Buttercup and her calf had to do the rest.

For a moment the little calf on the ground didn't move. Shocked and exhausted by its birth, it just lay there gathering strength. Then it jerked its back leg slightly, trying to free itself from what remained of the bag of waters – the transparent membrane which it had been living in for the past nine months.

"Come on, Buttercup!" Lucy said softly, for she knew the new mother cow was shocked and exhausted as well and needed to be gently encouraged. "You've got your baby now. Look after it."

After a moment, Buttercup turned her head to look at her calf. She moved round on the straw and bent her head to help the calf free itself from the bag. Then she began licking it slowly, rhythmically, lovingly. The little calf struggled, curled and turned, lifting its head towards its mother searchingly. It knew by instinct that somewhere nearby was comfort and nourishment; it just had to find it.

Slowly, slowly, as Buttercup licked and groomed her calf, this instinct told the young animal what it had to do next. It tried to get to its feet and collapsed – once, twice, three times. Then it tried pushing up with its hind legs first, and actually managed it. Staggering, feet splayed out at odd angles, it jerked its way round until it was facing the right direction, then it lurched towards Buttercup. Cow and calf greeted each other, noses together. Watching them with her heart in her mouth, Lucy felt her eyes fill up with tears again.

Lucy breathed a deep, deep sigh of relief and wiped the tears away on her shirt tails. Wearily, yawning all the time, she took off the shirt and rubber gloves. She looked out of the window – the storm seemed to have passed over them. The rain had stopped, the sky was clear and there was a full moon beaming over the roof of the farmhouse.

Buttercup, the most important job of her life done, knelt down on the straw. Her calf took unsteady steps around its mum, leaned against her and then slid to the floor too.

More tired than she'd ever been before, Lucy lowered herself to the ground and rested her head against a bale of straw. She'd watch the new calf – its name was Daisy, she decided – for a while longer, and then she'd go upstairs and sleep until her mum and dad came back.

Dimly, she could hear chicks cheeping in the background. "Bet you've all hatched now," she said, yawning deeply, "but I'm too tired to get up and look at you."

As Lucy spoke, her head dropped forward and she fell fast asleep.

Chapter Seven

"Darling! Wake up!"

Lucy opened her eyes. Her mum was bending over her, looking anxious. "Are you all right?"

"What's . . . what am I doing here?" Lucy asked, looking from her mum to her dad and back again.

"That's what we want to know!" said her dad. "We searched the farmhouse and then we came out here and found you fast asleep in the straw with a cow and a strange calf I've never seen before."

"Whatever's been going on?" her mum asked worriedly.

Lucy suddenly remembered everything and struggled to sit up. "Look what I've done!" she beamed, pointing at the new little calf which was feeding from its mother. "This is Daisy. All my own work!"

"Good heavens! When was *that* born?" her dad asked.

"In the middle of the night! Its hooves were stuck back, and I had to help Buttercup get her out!"

"Oh, dear," Lucy's mum sighed. "What a to-do. Mr Mack came down, did he?"

Lucy shook her head. "No! The phone lines were down. I couldn't reach him."

"Oh no!" Tim Tremayne said, while Julie Tremayne gave an exclamation of horror. "What did you . . . however did you manage, darling?"

"Oh, it was OK," Lucy said airily. "I've seen Dad do it loads of times. The hooves were wedged, so I just moved them a bit and Buttercup did the rest. But how's Kerry? Where is she now?"

"She's fast asleep," their mum said. "Your dad's put her to bed." She gave a laugh. "I think she's going to be quite a menace with that plastered leg. She's already bashed Podger on the nose with it."

"So what happened?" Lucy's dad said. "What else—" He heard a noise behind him and swung round. "Chicks! Where did they come from?"

"Freckles hatched them!" Lucy said. "I found her in the lane, sitting on a nest under a hedge – the eggs were just about to be washed away."

"I *thought* she'd gone broody!" Lucy's mum said.

Her dad looked over the edge of the cardboard box. "Chicks for sale. Going cheep!" he said, trotting out one of his favourite jokes.

Lucy and her mum laughed, and then Julie Tremayne ruffled her daughter's hair. "Come inside now, darling. We'll have a cup of tea and then you can go to bed. We'll *all* go to bed. We've had quite a night."

"But first I want to hear more about what happened here last night," Lucy's dad said. "Right from the beginning."

"Well," Lucy began. She got to her feet,

eager to tell everything. "The first thing was Mrs—"

"Morning!" Mrs Dodkins, wearing a bright pink woolly dressing gown, peered over the bottom half of the barn door. "All back safely, I see!"

"Yes," Julie Tremayne said, "and we're so sorry if we inconvenienced you at all. Your first day here too."

"Don't mention it!" Mrs Dodkins said airily. "I managed everything perfectly well."

Lucy stared at her, dumbstruck.

"It was no trouble at all," Mrs Dodkins went on. "As I believe I mentioned, I'm an experienced babysitter. We had a very quiet night, didn't we, Lucy?"

Lucy thought about it. Thought about rescuing Mrs Dotty from the churchyard in the middle of a storm, about finding Freckles and making her an incubator, about discovering Buttercup was in labour and delivering a calf on her own.

She breathed out deeply. "Yes, Mrs Dodkins," she said. "It was a *very* quiet night."

LUCY'S FARM 2
Lucy's Donkey Rescue

When Lucy meets a poor neglected donkey on the beach, she is desperate to help him. His horrible owner is so cruel.

Lucy knows that her parents will never agree to keeping another animal on the farm. Can Donald, a very clever donkey, prove that Hollybrook really does need him?

LUCY'S FARM 3
Lucy's Badger Cub

Lucy and her friend Beth enjoy watching the badgers in the woods. They are horrified to find one day that all the badgers have gone – except for one little cub.

But there are more mysteries down in the woods. Someone has been living in the old ruined cottage. Can Lucy discover what is going on – and save her little badger cub?

LUCY'S FARM 5
Lucy's Wild Pony

Lucy doesn't believe the spooky stories she hears about ghosts on the moors. Everyone knows that only wild ponies live up there!

Following a friend who has wandered too far on the moor, Lucy finds herself in great danger. But then a mysterious white pony appears . . .

Collect all the LUCY'S FARM books!

The prices shown below are correct at the time of going to press. However, Macmillan Publishers reserve the right to show new retail prices on covers which may differ from those previously advertised.

Mary Hooper

1. A Lamb for Lucy	0 330 36794 3	£2.99
2. Lucy's Donkey Rescue	0 330 36795 1	£2.99
3. Lucy's Badger Cub	0 330 36796 X	£2.99
4. A Stormy Night for Lucy	0 330 36797 8	£2.99
5. Lucy's Wild Pony	0 330 36798 6	£2.99
6. Lucy's Perfect Piglet	0 330 36799 4	£2.99

All Macmillan titles can be ordered at your local bookshop or are available by post from:

Books Service by Post
PO Box 29, Douglas, Isle of Man IM99 1BQ

Credit cards accepted. For details:
Telephone: 01624 675137
Fax: 01624 670923
E-mail: bookshop@enterprise.net

Free postage and packing in the UK.
Overseas customers: add £1 per book (paperback)
and £3 per book (hardback)